Hags on High
Headquarters

Squashed fly!
(Don't tell H.A.)

Other way   Over there
← This way   That way →

338 Euston Road, London NW1 3BH

ORCHARD BOOKS

Orchard Books Australia   Level 17/207 Kent Street, Sydney, NSW 2000

ISBN 978 1 84616 064 6

First published in 2009 by Orchard Books

Text © Hiawyn Oram 2009   Illustrations © Sarah Warburton 2009

The rights of Hiawyn Oram to be identified as the author and Sarah Warburton to be identified as the illustrator

of this work have been asserted by them in accordance

with the Copyright, Designs and Patents Act, 1988.

A CIP catalogue record for this book is availabe from the British Library.

Orchard Books is a division of Hachette Children's books,

an Hachette UK company.

www.hachette.co.uk

Printed in China

10 9 8 7 6 5 4 3 2 1

poached Cat!

Dinner! ME!

boiled witch!

Hiawyn Oram

Rumblewick
and the Dinner Dragons

Sarah Warburton

ORCHARD BOOKS

This is Rumblewick Spellwacker Mortimer B – cat to a witch who doesn't want to be one.

me

This is his witch, Haggy Aggy – the only witch in witchdom who wears pink, keeps off broomsticks and completely will not go out scaring anyone.

HA

And **NOW** she wants to do something no witchy witch would think of.

She wants to make friends with **DRAGONS**.

My best friend, Grimey

What is Rumblewick to do? Read his letters to his friend, Grimey, and see . . .

GRRRRRR

EEK!!

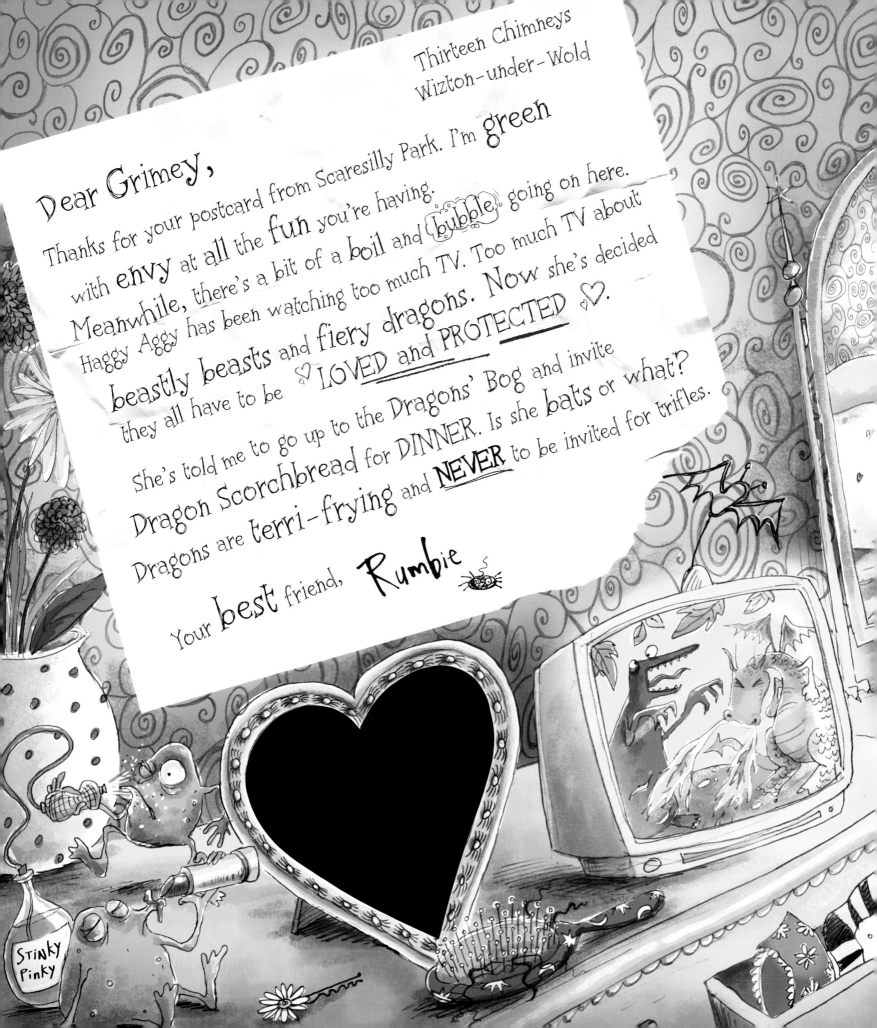

Thirteen Chimneys
Wizton-under-Wold

Dear Grimey,

Thanks for your postcard from Scaresilly Park. I'm **green** with **envy** at all the **fun** you're having.

Meanwhile, there's a bit of a *boil* and *bubble* going on here. Haggy Aggy has been watching too much TV. Too much TV about *beastly beasts* and *fiery dragons*. Now she's decided they all have to be ♡ LOVED and PROTECTED ♡.

She's told me to go up to the Dragons' Bog and invite Dragon Scorchbread for DINNER. Is she **bats** or what? Dragons are **terri-frying** and **NEVER** to be invited for trifles.

Your **best** friend, *Rumbie*

STINKY Pinky

Dear Rumbie,
    She's bats all right.
A DRAGON for dinner?
What will you COOK?
Or will he cook YOU?
If only she'd get on with
being the **scary** witch she
SHOULD be so you can get
on with being the **great**
witch's cat you ARE.
Anyway, look what I found
for you in the hotel spell
library!
    Use it and be safe, my
friend.
    Yours ever,
        Grimey

SHRIEKHARD HOTEL
SCARESILLY PARK

POST CARD
ADDRESS

1ST

Rumblewick
Spellwaker Mortimer B
Thirteen Chimneys

Wizton-under-Wold

PRINTED IN
W.U.W
Pub. by:-
haggette & hoggitt

A POCKET
BOOK OF
Dragons

SPELL TO BE-FRIENDLY THE TERRI-FRYING

Place a steaming cauldron of chopped shrigglewort and minced mysterytoe outside the terri-fryer's den. Hanging upside down, chant the following seven times:

DRAGONS AND ALL FIERY BEASTS

FROM NOW YOU WILL NOT BAKE ME

YOU'LL WELCOME EVERY MOVE I MAKE

A DISH YOU WILL NOT MAKE ME.

DRAGONS AND ALL FIERY BEASTS

YOU'LL HAVE NO PLANS TO EAT ME

YOU'LL WELCOME ME AS FRIEND NOT FOE

AND SAY YOU'RE GLAD TO MEET ME!

SMALL PRINT: If this spell does not work, don't worry—
you won't know because you'll have been lunch.

Grimey
Scares.....

Thirteen Chimneys
Wizton-under-Wold

Dear Grimey,

You are a TOTAL MOON for sending that spell.

I used it and it worked **brilliantly**. In fact, a bit <u>too</u> brilliantly.
Not **only** did Scorchbread say he'd like to come for dinner
but he asked if he could bring some <u>friends and family!</u>

Of course, Haggy Aggy said YES, so I've spent the
day preparing dinner for dragonzzz. While all **she's** been doing
is laying the table and thinking up GOING HOME PRESENTS
for her **'guests'!** Have you ever heard of anything more
<u>unwitchy</u> than this, because I haven't? Anyway, I've got to
get back to the kitchen. I'll write more when I can.

Yours, **Rumbie**

PS: Here is my Dinner for Dragonzzz.

RED HOT LAVA SAUCE

EYE BROWS

BAD-TEMPERED DRIPPING

Crafty Co-op

Receipt number 1313777

Eyeballs 7.98

Magic Beans 13.77

Ogre Feet 6.66

Comfrey 3.13

Thankyou for your custom
Have a GOOD SPELL

Thirteen Chimneys
Day after the Dragonzzz Dinner

Dear Grimey,
So much to tell, I hardly know where to begin.
Scorchbread arrived with his friend Gorjuss, his aunt Armatilda,
his grandfather Gorgonzoll AND his little cousin Nostrella.
Scorchbread was friendly enough, BUT THE REST OF THEM!
You should have seen the way they 👁 looked at me and
Haggy Aggy. As if they'd like US on their plates,
grilled with no gravy!
My fur was standing on end as I remembered . . . they hadn't been
de-terri-fried by your BE-FRIENDLY SPELL!

And my fur STAYED standing on end as it dawned on me . . . it was too late to do the spell now. I was right out of shrigglewort and mysterytoe, and Haggy Aggy was telling me to bring in the dinner – DOUBLE PRESTO.

And DOUBLE PRESTO wasn't just me serving that carefully prepared seven-course dinner. I wish you could have seen how fast those dragons ate. They shibbled and slobbled up every last tiddly tadpole of it – in less time than it takes to tell you about it.

And THEN they started banging the table and puff-roaring "MORE!".
When I explained there WAS no more because they'd already eaten
EVERYTHING and the cupboards were BARE, they started breathing
flicklets of fire and staring at Haggy Aggy and me with looks that said . . .
"Then we'll eat you . . . terri-fried and tossed up on toast."
Unfortunately, Haggy Aggy did not seem to notice.

"Oh RB," she gasped. "Isn't this just the **cosiest** thing? A whole lot of dragons to love ♡ and protect. And by the way, I've invited them to stay the night. Scorchbread, Gorgonzoll and Gorjuss can sleep in the broomstick shed. Armatilda can have the sofa and Nostrella will share your log basket."

All I could think of was YIKES and TRIPLE YIKES. How would 1 get a wink of shut-eye with a **dragon** in my bed? Especially one that hadn't been spelled into be-friendliness

AND WAS <u>STILL</u> HUNGRY?

As it turned out, that was the **least** of my worries.

YIKES x 3 !!

Midnight Beast !!

zzz

Almost as soon as she was under the covers,
Nostrella began to CRY — great wet puddly tears.
To my own surprise, I found my voice saying softly,
"What is it, Nostrella? What's the matter?"
"I don't like it here," she puddled.
"I want to go HOME."
At the word 'home', her tears went from puddle
to (pool) size. And I could see that if she didn't
stop crying soon we'd need waterwings
and a broomstick boat. I was at the window
in a flash, pointing at the moon.

"But look," I yelped. "You can't go anywhere. It's nearly midnight and we haven't had our Midnight Feast!" Her tears dried to a drizzle. "Feast?" she said, brightening. "BIG feast?"

"Well, maybe, sort of big," I stammered, remembering that unless I frittered some of Haggy Aggy's precious pet frogs, there was exactly ZILCHO to eat in the house.

"Then I want to go HOME," she cried and the puddling and pooling started again. So I did all I could do. I made up a Feast from THIN AIR.

Here is the menu, in case you ever find yourself in such a soggy situation.

Story Pie

STROKE OF MIDNIGHT
"The cupboard is bare"
MIDNIGHT FEAST

weeeeee

Game Soup

Hopscotch

Well, that did it, all right.

Not only did Nostrella stop crying, she woke up the other dragons and made them join our 'FEAST'! And they had so much 'feastly fun,' they stopped looking at Haggy Aggy and me terri-fryingly. In fact, it's as clear as new moonlight, we are their NEW BEST FRIENDS! Of course, Haggy Aggy couldn't be more thrilled.

"Oh RB!" she keeps saying. "All this by kindness and not a spell in sight."

And in moments like these, I see what a megalight of marvelwockery she can be ... Even if she is a bit bats in the belfry, invites dragons for dinner and refuses to scare anyone's socks off. Hope you'll be home soon.

Your best friend, Rumbie